First published in Switzerland under the title *Phillibert fliegt!*

First published in the United States, Great Britain, Canada, Australia, and New Zealand
in 2003 by North-South Books, an imprint of Nord-Süd Verlag AG, Gossau Zürich, Switzerland.

Distributed in the United States by North-South Books Inc., New York.

Library of Congress Cataloging-in-Publication Data is available.
A CIP catalogue record for this book is available from The British Library.
ISBN 0-7358-1829-0 (trade edition) 10 9 8 7 6 5 4 3 2 1
ISBN 0-7358-1830-4 (library edition) 10 9 8 7 6 5 4 3 2 1
Printed in Belgium

For more information about our books, and the authors and artists
who create them, visit our web site: www.northsouth.com

Filbert Flies

by Karl Rühmann

Illustrated by Rolf Siegenthaler

Translated by Marianne Martens

North-South Books
New York / London

One beautiful morning, Filbert soared high across the deep blue Antarctic sky. He was in a hurry and flew as fast as his wings would carry him.

He didn't notice a big seagull flying behind him.

“Excuse me, excuse me!” screeched the seagull. “What do you think you are doing, passing me? You aren’t allowed to do that.”

“Why not?” asked Filbert, without slowing down.

“Because you are a penguin, that’s why. Everyone knows that penguins can’t fly!”

“They can’t?” asked Filbert.

Just then he caught sight of a group of penguins, waddling awkwardly on the ice below. Not a single one of them was trying to fly. “Good grief—how embarrassing,” thought Filbert.

And crash-landed in the snow.

Sad and ashamed, Filbert moped on the ice. How could I forget that penguins can't fly? he thought. I was doing fine until that seagull reminded me. Filbert was very upset, and a little angry, too. The more he thought about it, the angrier he got. Soon he was so cross, he tried to tear out one of his tail feathers. But with his short beak, he couldn't reach one.

A little seal slid across the snow to him. “What’s the matter? You look so sad.”

Filbert sighed. “I was so happy flying along. Then I realized that I can’t fly—I’m just a penguin.”

"What do you mean, '*just* a penguin?'" the seal cried. "Who cares if you can't fly? Think of all the other things you can do."

"Like what?" sniffed Filbert.

"Like sliding on your rear down the slope."

Filbert wiped the tears from his eyes.

“And no one can beat you in races with the white whale.”
Filbert stopped sniffling.

“And you’re a world champion skater. All the girl penguins love to watch you doing ice dances.” The seal winked and nudged Filbert in the ribs.

Filbert listened eagerly.

"And you are the most elegant waddler around. Look at your beautiful black-and-white coat—very stylish indeed. I wish I had one, too."

"Well, maybe you're right," said Filbert, feeling much happier. "You've helped me a lot. Thank you so much."

The seal continued, "Just remember . . ."

". . . you can do anything you want to, if you just set your mind to it." And before Filbert could say a word, the seal pushed off from the ice and flew into the air.

Soon Filbert could see only a tiny dot in the Antarctic sky.

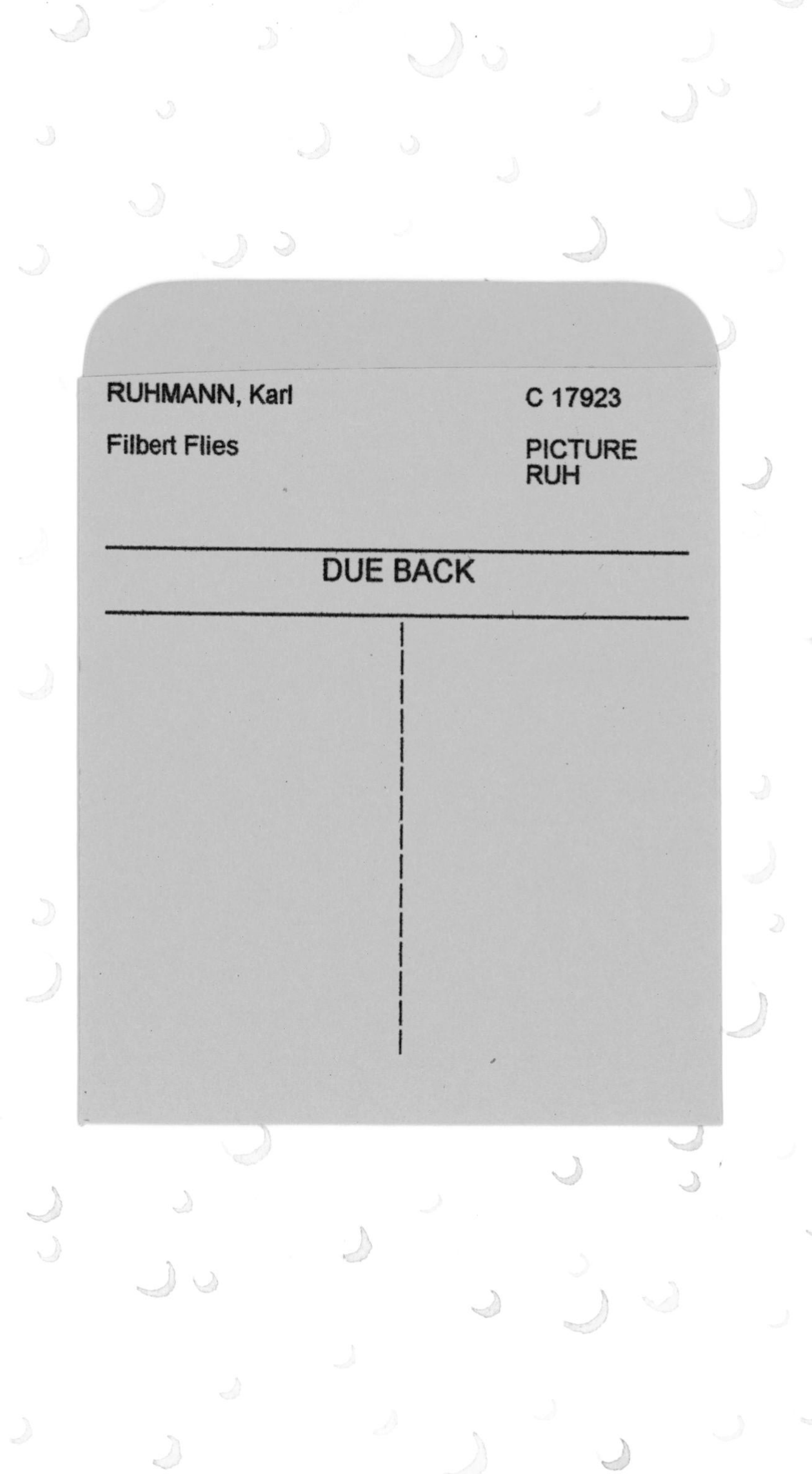

RUHMANN, Karl

Filbert Flies

C 17923

PICTURE
RUH

DUE BACK